Hillary Squeak's
DREADFUL DRAGON

Story and Pictures
by JOAN ELIZABETH GOODMAN

A GOLDEN BOOK • NEW YORK
Western Publishing Company, Inc., Racine, Wisconsin 53404

The sun was setting behind Meadowtown when Hillary Squeak awoke from a snooze beside her favorite fishing hole.

"Golly!" she said. "I've overslept! It will soon be night. I don't want to walk through Ravenswood in the dark."

Hillary grabbed her fishing gear and headed for home as fast as she could. Down the banks of Beaver Creek she raced, under Cross Creek Bridge, past the Falls, around Little Pond, until she came to the woods.

"Too late! It's already dark here." Hillary shuddered. "Maybe I *should* have tried crossing Briar Patch."

Hillary took a deep breath and stepped into the gloom of Ravenswood. Giant oak trees towered above her, inky against the violet sky. She tiptoed along the dark, shadowy path.

"Wolves could be hiding in those shadows," she thought. "Big shaggy wolves with huge fangs. They could leap out and gobble me up!"

A twig snapped. Hillary whirled around. Nothing was there. She hurried on, trembling with fright.

The wind made eerie music as it whistled through the oak trees and rustled the underbrush.

"Maybe there's a giant snake around here," thought Hillary. "One that only comes out at night. It could be in the bushes now, just watching and waiting."

Hillary's heart pounded as she ran faster through the deepest, darkest part of Ravenswood. She rounded a bend in the path and froze in her tracks.

"A DRAGON!" she gasped.

There it was, more horrible than wolves or snakes—a monstrous, fire-breathing dragon! Smoke billowed from its mouth. Lightning flashed from its orange eyes. Long scaly arms reached out to grab Hillary.

"AAAGH!" she screamed, and she was off like a shot, with the dragon close behind.

It snatched at her with its terrible long claws. Its smoky breath choked her. Its long snaky tail tripped her. Hillary plunged onward. Soon she could see the edge of the woods. Hillary gathered her strength, and, in a final burst of speed, she broke free of Ravenswood and the dragon.

She ran until she arrived, shaky and breathless, at Lucy Softpaws's front door.

"Help! Help!" squeaked Hillary. "The dragon is chasing me!"

"Mercy!" said Lucy. "A real dragon?"

"It almost caught me and ate me. It has terrible long claws and fire shooting out of its mouth!"

"Now that you mention it," said Lucy, "stinky smoke has been coming out of Ravenswood."

"We've got to run for it!" said Hillary. "The dragon will burn down Meadowtown."

"I'll just pack a few things," said Lucy.

"There's no time!" said Hillary. "We must warn the others." She dragged Lucy up Foxglove Highway toward Pondside Lane.

They hadn't gone far when they ran into Frankie
Pudwoggle. He was out for an evening stroll, dribbling his
basketball.

"The dragon is coming!" shouted Hillary. "Run for your
life!"

"I'm not running away from any dumb old dragon," said
Frankie.

"It's not dumb," said Hillary. "It almost ate me. Now it's burning down Meadowtown!"

"And it smells awful," said Lucy.

"Sounds almost as bad as some of the teams I've played," said Frankie. "Let's get Edward Hopper in on this."

"Yes," said Hillary. "We've got to warn him."

They all rushed over to tell Edward about the dragon. They found him dusting his buttons.

"The dragon is coming!" screamed Hillary. "RUN!"

"A dragon!" said Edward. "How interesting. Where did you see it?"

"It tried to tear me to pieces in Ravenswood," said Hillary. "Now it's burning down all of Meadowtown. We've got to run while we can."

"I've never seen a dragon," said Edward. "I'd better photograph it for my collection." Edward grabbed his camera and raced out the door. Frankie, Lucy, and Hillary hurried after him.

"The dragon is a TERRIBLE MONSTER," said Hillary. "You can't photograph a monster. It will eat us all!"

"Don't worry so," said Edward. "We'll be careful."

"No one ever believes me!" said Hillary.

Soon they came to Ravenswood.

"There's that awful smell," said Lucy. "Maybe we should go home."

"Something seems to be burning," said Edward.

"I told you!" said Hillary. "The dragon is burning down Ravenswood."

"Let me at it," said Frankie. "I'll go it one-on-one."

"Then you go first," said Lucy.

"Good plan," said Edward.

They crept single file, behind Frankie, into the murky depths of Ravenswood.

"What are we doing here?" Hillary moaned. "We should be running the other way."

But on they went, deeper and deeper into darkest Ravenswood.

High-pitched shrieks were coming from the woods just ahead of them. Everyone stopped, their hearts thumping.

"Sounds like the dragon is eating the Squirrel clan," whispered Frankie.

"And we'll be next!" said Hillary.

"The smoke is thicker," said Edward. "We must be getting close."

"Maybe we are too close," said Lucy.

"We've g-g-got t-t-to st-st-stand f-f-firm," said Frankie.

"THERE IT IS!" yelled Hillary.

"WHERE?" asked Lucy.

"There!" Hillary spun around to point out the dragon.

"That's the Squirrels' oak tree," said Lucy.

Hillary blinked, rubbed her eyes, and stared and stared.

"Looks like they're having a cookout," said Edward.

"That must have been the fire-breathing part," said Hillary in amazement.

"They're burning acorns," said Lucy. "No wonder it's so stinky."

"It's not so bad," said Frankie.

"Those branches were the claws, and these roots were the tail," said Hillary. "I'm such a noodlehead. I was so afraid of the dark that I turned the Squirrels' barbecue into a dragon. I always get so carried away!"

"We all get carried away sometimes," said Lucy. "And it certainly smells like a dragon."

"Pity," said Edward. "My collection could have used a dragon photograph."

"Next time you need a dragon slayer," said Frankie, "count on me."

"I'm lucky to have such good friends to save me from my imaginary dragons," said Hillary.

Everyone had a good laugh over Hillary's dragon as they strolled home through sleepy Meadowtown, and then they said, "Good night."